This Little Hippo
book belongs to:

HOTEL

Scholastic Children's Books,
Commonwealth House, 1-19 New Oxford Street,
London WC1A 1NU, UK
a division of Scholastic Ltd

London - New York - Toronto - Sydney - Auckland
Mexico City - New Delhi - Hong Kong

First published by Scholastic Ltd, 1999

Developed from the
original books by Michelle Cartlidge.
Story adapted by Caryn Jenner. Illustrated by Colin Twinn.

2 4 6 8 10 9 7 5 3 1

ISBN 0 590 11373 9

Printed in China

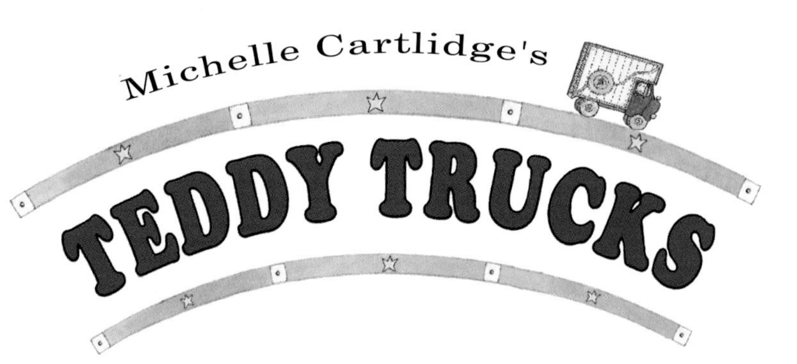

Rosie's Day Out

It was the end of the week.
The Teddy Truck drivers were
relaxing at Rosie's Café.

"It's nice to have an extra day off work," said Wilson.
"It's brilliant!" said Jacko.

Just then, Rosie brought in a tray full of jam buns. “Fresh from the oven,” she said.

“You do work hard, Rosie,” said Bella.

“I’m looking forward to my day off,” Rosie replied.

“I have an idea!” said Wilson. “Let’s take Rosie out for a day in the country!”

"Great idea!" said the others.
"Woof!" barked Nutley.
"We could all bring treats
for a picnic," said Bella.

“Let’s visit Boss Bear at his holiday caravan,” said Jacko.

They all made plans for their trip to the country.

The next day, everyone met outside Rosie's Café.

"I'm so excited!" said Rosie.

They all brought goodies for the picnic.

"I've brought some fresh eggs," said Gerry.

"How will we eat raw eggs on a picnic?" asked Jacko.

"Oh," said Gerry. "I hadn't thought of that."

The three trucks set off. Rosie and Bella were first.

"Is it far to Boss Bear's caravan?" Rosie asked.

"We'll have to check the map," said Bella. "It's near a village called Little Gradely."

The bears soon left the town behind them, as they drove into the beautiful green countryside.

"How about our picnic?" called Jacko over the radio.

"We're hungry back here," added Wilson.

The teddies found a pretty spot near a stream and parked the trucks. They were all hungry, and soon the food was gone – except for Gerry's raw eggs.

After lunch, they dozed on the grass.

"Is someone splashing me?" asked Jacko suddenly.

"That's rain," said Bella.

Quickly, they packed up the remains of the picnic, and set off again for Boss Bear's caravan.

In the first truck, Rosie studied the map. “I can’t find Little Gradely,” she said.

Bella signalled for the trucks to stop in a lay-by.

“We’re lost,” she told the other teddies.

"We'll have to camp for the night," said Wilson.

"But we haven't got a tent," Jacko pointed out.

"We'll have to make one," said Bella.

"What fun!" said Rosie.

Bella found plastic sheets and tarpaulins in her truck. She and Wilson and Jacko made the tent, while Rosie and Gerry collected wood for a campfire. At last, the tent was ready, and a small fire was burning.

"I'm really enjoying my trip to the country," said Rosie. "It's even stopped raining."

“I’m hungry again,” said Jacko. “But there’s nothing left to eat.”

Rosie jumped to her feet. “I’ll cook Gerry’s eggs for supper! It’s just as well I brought my frying pan.”

Gerry grinned. “I knew those eggs would be useful.”

“Delicious!” Wilson said later. He patted his tummy.

“I’m sorry you had to make supper on your day off from work, Rosie,” said Bella.

“I don’t mind,” Rosie said with a smile. “It’s fun cooking on the campfire.”

“I have an idea,” said Jacko. “Let’s have a sing-song round the campfire.”

Rosie began to sing: “One man went to mow a meadow . . .”

The others joined in.

"Excuse me!" came a voice from the other side of the hedge. The teddies stopped singing. "Would you mind keeping the noise down, please," said the voice. "I'm trying to sleep."

"That sounds like Boss Bear," said Gerry.

It was Boss Bear! Everyone was surprised to see him.

"We were coming to visit you," Bella told him. "But we couldn't find your caravan."

"It's over there, in the next field," said Boss Bear.

"Do you want to join our sing-song, Boss?" said Jacko.

Boss Bear cleared his throat. "I'd be delighted."

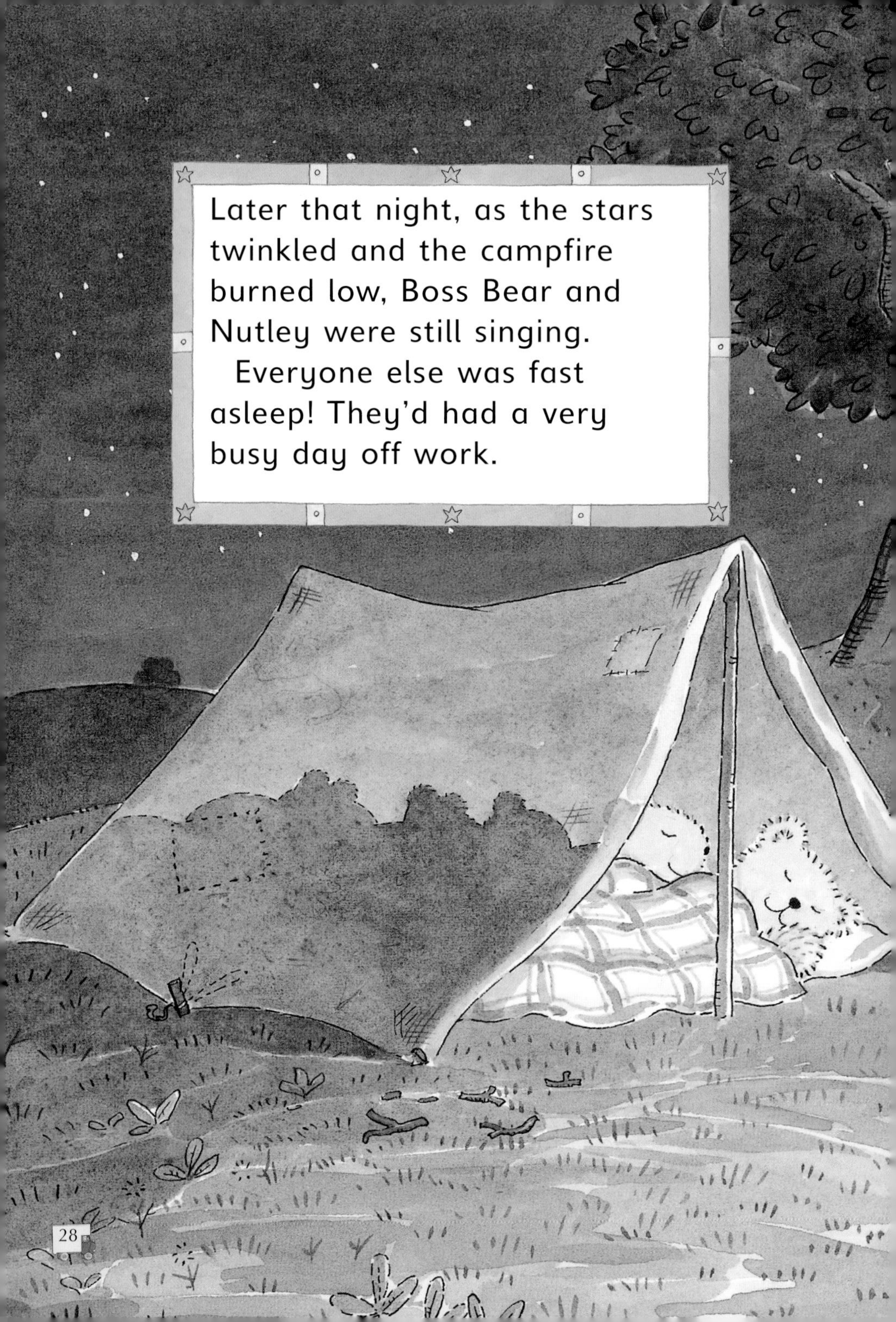

Later that night, as the stars twinkled and the campfire burned low, Boss Bear and Nutley were still singing.

Everyone else was fast asleep! They'd had a very busy day off work.

HOTEL